My dear Rose,

Our stay on the Planet of the Overhearers helped me understand the importance of finding new ways to fight the Snake's negative influence. On each new world, he becomes more crafty and harder to overcome. We narrowly avoided a catastrophe—I almost fought with Fox! But we learned an important lesson: not all communication is spoken.

Even if Fox always teases me about them, these letters are the mirror of my soul, its way of expression, and my greatest happiness. They remind me every day of the importance of our voyage: nothing must ever prevent those who love each other from sharing their feelings.

And while spoken communication can be misunderstood, writing fires up our imaginations and transports our hearts.

The Little Prince

First American edition published in 2013 by Graphic Universe™.

Le Petit Prince™

based on the masterpiece by Antoine de Saint-Exupéry

Graphic Universe™
A division of Lerner Publishing Group, Inc.
241 First Avenue North
Minneapolis, MN 55401 U.S.A.

Website address: www.lernerbooks.com

Library of Congress Cataloging-in-Publication Data

Benedetti, Hervé.
[Planète des Carapodes. English]
The planet of the Tortoise Driver / story by Hervé Benedetti and Nicolas Robin ; design and illustrations by Élyum Studio ; adaptation by Guillaume Dorison ; translation, Anne Collins Smith and Owen Smith. — 1st American ed.
p. cm. — (The little prince ; #08)
ISBN 978-0-7613-8758-9 (lib. bdg. : alk. paper)
1. Graphic novels. I. Robin, Nicolas. II. Dorison, Guillaume. III. Smith, Anne Collins. IV. Smith, Owen (Owen M.) V. Saint-Exupéry, Antoine de, 1900—1944. Petit Prince. VI. Élyum Studio. VII. Petit Prince (Television program) VIII. Title.
PZ7.7.B445Pl 2013
741.5'944—dc23 2012028304

Manufactured in the United States of America
1 — DP — 12/31/12

THE NEW ADVENTURES
BASED ON THE MASTERPIECE BY ANTOINE DE SAINT-EXUPÉRY

The Little Prince

THE PLANET OF THE TORTOISE DRIVER

Based on the animated series and an original story by Hervé Benedetti and Nicolas Robin

Design: Élyum Studio
Story: Guillaume Dorison
Artistic Direction: Didier Poli
Art: Audrey Bussi
Backgrounds: Isa Python
Coloring: Nolwenn Feliot
Editing: Didier Poli
Editorial Consultant: Didier Convard

Translation: Anne and Owen Smith

Graphic Universe™ • Minneapolis • New York

THE LITTLE PRINCE

The Little Prince has extraordinary gifts. His sense of wonder allows him to discover what no one else can see. The Little Prince can communicate with all the beings in the universe, even the animals and plants. His powers grow over the course of his adventures.

The Prince's uniform:
When he transforms into the uniform of a prince, he is more agile and quick. When faced with difficult situations, the Little Prince also uses a sword that lets him sketch and bring to life anything from his imagination.

His sketchbook:
When he is not in his Prince's clothing, the Little Prince carries a sketchbook. When he blows on the pages, they take wing and form objects that he'll find very useful. Like his sword, it's powered by stardust collected on his travels.

FOX

A grouch, a trickster, and, so he says, interested only in his next meal, Fox is in reality the Little Prince's best friend. As such, he is always there to give him help but also just as much to help him to grow and to learn about the world.

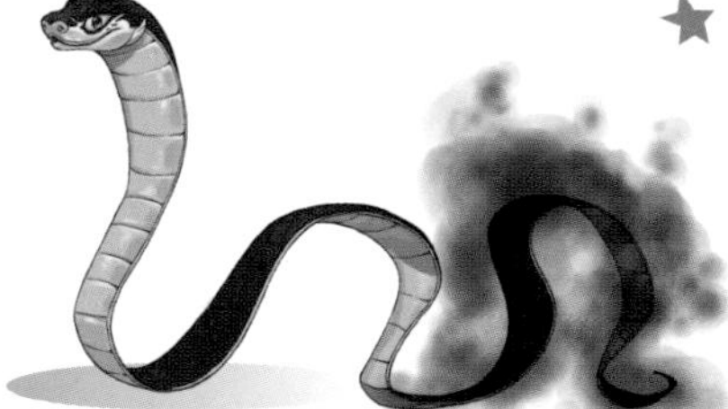

THE SNAKE

Even though the Little Prince still does not know exactly why, there can be no doubt that the Snake has set his mind to plunging the entire universe into darkness! And to accomplish his goal, this malicious being is ready to use any form of deception. However, the Snake never takes action himself. He prefers to bring out the wickedness in those beings he has chosen to bite, tempting them to put their own worlds in danger.

THE GLOOMIES

When people who have been "bitten" by the Snake have completely destroyed their own planets, they become Gloomies, slaves to their Snake master. The Gloomies act as a group and carry out the Snake's most vile orders so he can get the better of the Little Prince!

I WISH...I COULD...LIVE MY OWN LIFE...

THE CITY OF QWERTUS, THE GOLDEN WEEK FESTIVAL...
SO MY WIFE ASKED IF I WAS IN SHAPE...AND I SAID, "WHAT SHAPE DO YOU WANT ME IN?"

I THOUGHT WE COULD WRITE TO EACH OTHER, BY CARAPOST. HERE'S MY FIRST LETTER.
OH, GRAMM... WHAT A LOVELY IDEA! I PROMISE I'LL WRITE BACK AS SOON AS I GET HOME.
GRAMM! WHAT ARE YOU DOING, DEAR?
NOTHING, MOM... I'LL BE RIGHT THERE!

SEVERAL MONTHS LATER . . .

A NICE WELCOME FOR ONCE!

WHAT ARE YOU TALKING ABOUT? LOOK AROUND--WE CAN'T GET OUT!

I PROMISED NOT TO SULK OR COMPLAIN, BUT I REFUSE TO SAVE THIS PLANET IF I HAVE TO ANSWER ALL THESE LETTERS!

HEY, COME BACK! I WAS ONLY JOKING. DON'T LEAVE ME HERE BY MYSELF!

I FOUND AN EXIT DOWN AT THE BOTTOM... LET'S GO!

WHOA!

HEY, THEY'RE HERE!

IT'S BEEN SO LONG. WE WERE STARTING TO WORRY...
ALL THAT MATTERS IS THAT YOU'RE HERE. WE'RE SAVED!

FOR ONCE, OUR REPUTATION HAS PRECEDED US!

BUT WHERE'S YOUR CARAPODE? HOW WILL YOU CARRY ALL THE MAIL?
WAIT, YOU'RE NOT DRESSED LIKE CARAPOSTAL WORKERS...

CARA-WHAT?

CAN'T YOU SEE THEY'RE NOT CARAPOSTAL WORKERS?

THEN THEY MUST BE MAIL THIEVES, AMSTRAM...
MAYBE THAT'S WHY WE'RE NOT GETTING MAIL ANYMORE!

HERE WE GO AGAIN!

MY FELLOW KESKIS! IF THEY WERE MAIL THIEVES, HOW COULD THEY TAKE OUR LETTERS ACROSS THE GREAT SALT DESERT WITHOUT A CARAPODE?

THIS BOY'S RED MINI-CARAPODE THING WOULDN'T LAST THIRTY SECONDS ON THE WHITE SALT FLATS! HE'S NO THIEF, JUST A TROUBLEMAKER.

FOX IS NOT A THING OR A CARA-SOMETHING. HE'S MY FRIEND... AND WE'RE HERE TO SAVE YOUR PLANET!

OH REALLY? THEN YOU'LL HAVE TO TELL ME MORE. COME ON! YOU CAN TELL ME ABOUT IT WHILE I SHOW YOU AROUND.

GLAD TO MEET YOU, LITTLE PRINCE, AND YOU TOO, FOX.

I UNDERSTAND WHY YOU'VE COME HERE, BUT IT DOESN'T MAKE SENSE. OUR PLANET ISN'T IN ANY DANGER--THERE'S NO WAR AND NO CONFLICT, LET ALONE AN EVIL SNAKE.

PERFECT! WE MUST HAVE GOTTEN THE ADDRESS WRONG. CAN WE GO NOW?

BUT WHY IS THERE A PROBLEM WITH THE MAIL? IS THERE A STRIKE?

NOTHING LIKE THAT, IT'S MUCH MORE SERIOUS...

YOU'RE IN AZERTUS, ONE OF THE FIVE BIG CITIES WHERE THE KESKIS LIVE...

BUT WE'RE ISOLATED, SEPARATED FROM OUR BROTHERS AND SISTERS.

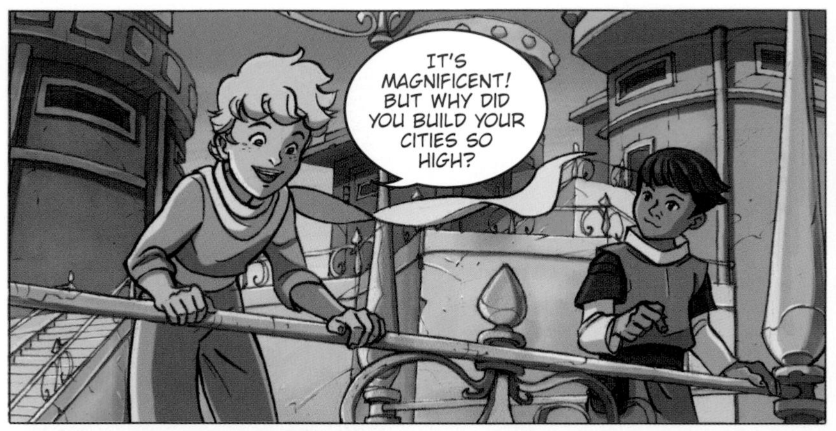
IT'S MAGNIFICENT! BUT WHY DID YOU BUILD YOUR CITIES SO HIGH?

WHAT YOU SEE BEFORE YOU IS NO ORDINARY COUNTRYSIDE...

IT'S A DESERT OF WHITE SALT, AND IT MEANS DEATH TO ANYONE WHO SETS FOOT ON IT.

THE SUN KEEPS THE WHITE SALT PERPETUALLY HOT. IT GIVES OFF WAVES OF HEAT THAT NO LIVING BEING CAN SURVIVE. EXCEPT THE GREAT TORTOISES--THE CARAPODES
ONLY THE CARAPODES CAN TRAVEL BETWEEN CITIES, EXCEPT DURING THE COLD SEASON. THEN, FOR ONE WEEK ONLY, WE CAN CROSS THE DESERT ON FOOT.

SO THE CARAPODES MUST BE REALLY IMPORTANT TO YOU.
YES--THEY TRANSPORT THE CARAPOST, THE POSTAL SERVICE THAT DISTRIBUTES THE MAIL AMONG THE FIVE BIG CITIES.

BUT FOR SEVERAL WEEKS NOW, THERE'S BEEN NO CARAPOST. OUR MAIL HASN'T BEEN PICKED UP, AND WE HAVEN'T RECEIVED ANY LETTERS FROM THE OTHER CITIES!

AND I HAVEN'T EVEN GOTTEN MY INVITATION TO THE GREAT JOKE COMPETITION! CAN YOU HELP ME, LITTLE PRINCE? I BET YOU HAVE PLENTY OF MAGICAL POWERS...

HOW DARE YOU, AMSTRAM? IS YOUR SILLY COMPETITION THE MOST IMPORTANT THING IN THE WORLD?

YOUR SON HAS BEEN WAITING EVERY DAY FOR A LETTER FROM HIS SWEETHEART!

FEAR IS GRIPPING THE WHOLE CITY, AND ALL YOU CAN THINK ABOUT IS YOURSELF!

UM, MAY I INTRODUCE MY WIFE PIKDAM AND MY SON GRAMM...

GET BACK IN THE HOUSE, GRAMM. SOMEONE'S GOT TO BE THE GROWN-UP HERE.

DON'T MIND HER. SHE'S ALWAYS A BIT CRANKY.
I SEE.

SCARY...SHE MUST HAVE BEEN BITTEN BY THE SNAKE!

IT'S OUR FAULT, MA'AM. WE WERE IN DANGER AND AMSTRAM CAME TO OUR RESCUE.
I KNOW ALL THAT. JUST TELL ME IF YOU CAN HELP US OR NOT...

WE CAN ONLY SEE OUR FRIENDS AND FAMILY A FEW DAYS OUT OF THE YEAR. WHEN WE DON'T HEAR FROM THEM BY CARAPOST, WE CAN'T HELP FEELING THAT SOMETHING TERRIBLE HAS HAPPENED TO THEM.

PIKDAM, I DIDN'T KNOW...

DON'T WORRY. FOX AND I WILL INVESTIGATE AND FIND OUT WHAT'S WRONG.

THE SNAKE IS BECOMING MORE AND MORE VILE, FOX. ON THIS PLANET, HE'S NOT JUST INTERFERING WITH COMMUNICATION. HE'S TRYING TO TAKE AWAY THE PEOPLE'S HOPE. ONCE DESPAIR SETS IN, EVIL IS SURE TO FOLLOW. WE MUST BRING BACK THE CARAPOST AT ANY COST!

IF WE COULD FLY ABOVE THE DESERT, WE'D BE ABLE TO FIND THE CARAPODES, RIGHT?
YES, BUT ONLY THE CARAPODES CAN WALK ON THE WHITE SALT.

MY NOTEBOOK CAN BE VERY USEFUL...ALL I NEED IS A GUIDE!

CARAPODES IN SIGHT!
THEY'RE MOVING AT QUITE A CARA-PACE.
OH. HAR HAR.
IT'S A HERD OF WILD CARAPODES! ONLY THE CONDUCTOR KNOWS HOW TO TAME THEM.
THEY'RE AMAZING!
BUT WHERE'S THE ONE WE WANT?
NOT FAR AWAY, I THINK. WHEN ONE CARAPODE IS IN TROUBLE, THE OTHERS COME TO HELP.

ARE THEY GOOD TO EAT?

MAYBE WITH A BIT OF CARA-MEL...

LOOK! IS THAT THE ONE?
YES! HE'S THE ONE CARRYING THE CARAPOST.

IS HE SUPPOSED TO BE STANDING STILL?

ABSOLUTELY NOT. SOMETHING'S WRONG...

SHOULD WE GO RIGHT IN?
I'M NOT SURE...

I MIGHT HAVE AN IDEA.
THIS IS NO TIME TO WRITE TO YOUR ROSE!

WE CAN SEE HOW FAST YOUR POSTAL SERVICE WORKS-- HA HA HA!

PFFT! WE'RE LOST IN THE MIDDLE OF THE DESERT, WITHOUT A BITE TO EAT, WITH A COMEDIAN WHO ISN'T FUNNY AND A PRINCE WHO WANTS TO BE A POSTAL INSPECTOR!

THERE WE GO!

HELP HAS ARRIVED FOR ME AT LAST! GREETINGS, I'M PHILATELLO.

THANKS FOR THE WARM WELCOME, BUT I THINK YOU'VE GOT IT BACKWARD... ***WE'RE*** THE ONES WHO NEED ***YOUR*** HELP!

IF I UNDERSTAND YOU CORRECTLY, YOU'RE NOT BRINGING A NEW CONDUCTOR...
CONDUCTOR? OH, YOU HAVE AN ELECTRICAL PROBLEM?
AAARGH. I THINK I'D RATHER BE WITH THE SNAKE...

AMSTRAM IS FROM AZERTUS. THE PEOPLE THERE ARE VERY ANXIOUS FOR THEIR CARAPOST.

AND SO THEY SHOULD BE, MY BOY. NEVER HAS THERE BEEN SUCH A DELAY IN THE HISTORY OF THE CARAPOST.
YOU SEE, WE HAVE NO PILOT. WITHOUT A PILOT, THE CARAPODE WON'T MOVE, LEAVING THE CARAPOST AT A STANDSTILL. AND WITHOUT THE CARAPOST, THIS PLANET IS DOOMED!

WHY CAN'T ***YOU*** GET THIS BEAST MOVING AGAIN?

BECAUSE NO AMOUNT OF TRAINING CAN MAKE A PERSON A CONDUCTOR. IT REQUIRES COURAGE AND PATIENCE, BUT MOST OF ALL, YOU HAVE TO BE BORN WITH A NATURAL CONNECTION TO WILD CARAPODES. THERE'S NO BETTER CONDUCTOR THAN AROBASE, BUT ONE NIGHT HE DISAPPEARED WITHOUT A TRACE.

HE MUST HAVE GONE TO SING CARA-OKE! HA HA HA!

HA HA! THAT'S FUNNY! WE COULD USE AN ENTERTAINER LIKE YOU ON BOARD.

PHILATELLO, CAN YOU SHOW US WHERE AROBASE WORKED? MAYBE WE'LL FIND SOME CLUES THERE...

IF YOU'D LIKE, BUT I DOUBT YOU'LL FIND ANYTHING. WE'VE ALREADY GONE THROUGH IT WITH A FINE-TOOTH COMB.

AREN'T YOU COMING, AMSTRAM?

NO, PLEASE GO ON WITHOUT ME. THINKING UP JOKES WORE ME OUT.

THERE'S SOMETHING FISHY ABOUT AMSTRAM...
YOU'RE IMAGINING THINGS. HE'S HERE TO HELP HIS PEOPLE, ISN'T HE?

YOU CAN'T MISS IT! IT'S RIGHT AT THE END OF THE BRIDGE.
YOU'RE NOT COMING WITH US?

WHAT FOR? IT WOULDN'T DO ANY GOOD.
BESIDES, I'M ON DUTY. I CAN'T BE AWAY FROM MY POST. GOOD LUCK.

GULP...I KNEW IT! I'VE BEEN OUTFOXED AGAIN. WHY DO THESE THINGS KEEP HAPPENING TO ME?
GET A GRIP, FOX...PRETEND IT'S A SWING!

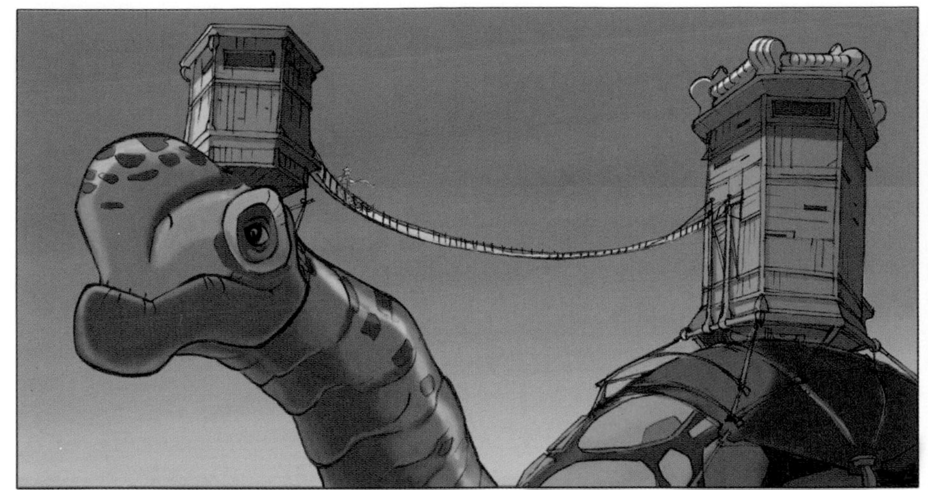

PHEW... NEVER AGAIN...

HEY, WHAT'S THAT?

THE CACA... CAPA...
...THE CARAPODES!

WHAT COULD POSSIBLY MAKE THEM STAMPEDE?

THERE HAS TO BE ANOTHER WAY... SOMETHING MUST BE FRIGHTENING THEM, BUT WHAT COULD IT BE?

TO TRUMPET AWAY SUCH A SHRILL SOUND...

...THERE'S NOTHING BETTER THAN AN ELEPHANT!

BRAAOOOOOM MAAOOOOM

NYARK NYARK NYARK
BRAAOOOOOM MAAOOOOM

BRAAOOOOOM MAAOOOOM

OOF...
SEEING GLOOMIES HERE PROVES THAT THE SNAKE DOESN'T WANT US TO FIND AROBASE. LET'S NOT WASTE ANY MORE TIME!

AROBASE LEFT A LONG TIME AGO. WHAT DO YOU HOPE TO FIND HERE?

A CLUE TO WHERE HE WENT AND WHY HE LEFT.

I HAVE A BETTER IDEA. SINCE YOU CAN COMMUNICATE WITH ANIMALS, WHY DON'T YOU JUST TALK TO THE CARAPODE YOURSELF AND ASK HIM TO START MOVING?

IT'S NOT THAT SIMPLE, FOX. I DON'T THINK AROBASE COULD "TALK" WITH THE CARAPODE... THEY HAD AN EMOTIONAL CONNECTION. THERE'S NO WAY TO REPLACE THAT!

THERE MUST BE SOMETHING HERE THAT PHILATELLO MISSED.

SO TELL ME, WHOSE JOKES DO YOU PREFER, MINE OR AMSTRAM'S?

OH NO, HELP...

FOX!

ARE YOU ALL RIGHT?
WHEW, I CAUSED A CARA-LANCHE!

YOU'RE BRILLIANT, FOX!
I KNOW.

HOW DID YOU KNOW THERE WAS SOMETHING BACK THERE?

THERE MUST BE SOME WAY TO OPEN IT...
MAYBE WITH A CARA-PULT?

HUMMMF!

SHADOW PUPPETS?

IT'S...IT'S AMAZING! IT SHOWS HOW AROBASE AND HIS CARAPODE WORK TOGETHER!
IS HE HIDING IN THERE?

LOOK, HERE'S SOMETHING ELSE...

IT'S A FLYER FOR THE CIRCUS OF QWERTUS! SO, AROBASE HAD A SECRET...
QWERTUS? ISN'T AMSTRAM'S JOKE COMPETITION BEING HELD THERE?
THIEVES! I'VE CAUGHT YOU RED-HANDED!

WHILE YOU WERE DISTRACTING ME BY RIFLING THIS CABIN, YOUR ACCOMPLICE WAS TRYING TO STEAL THIS LETTER!
HEY! NO NEED TO BRING OUT THE CARA-BINES! THIS LETTER IS ADDRESSED TO ME. IT'S MY INVITATION TO THE JOKE COMPETITION!

NO ONE BUT THE CARAPOST CAN DELIVER LETTERS!

IT'S NOT AMSTRAM'S FAULT. HE THOUGHT HE WAS DOING THE RIGHT THING BY FOLLOWING MY INSTRUCTIONS.
I NEEDED THIS LETTER TO FIND AROBASE!

HOW IS AN INVITATION TO A JOKE COMPETITION SUPPOSED TO SAVE OUR CARAPOST?
WHAT'S HE TALKING ABOUT?

IF I'M RIGHT, AROBASE LEFT TO JOIN THE CIRCUS DURING THE JOKE COMPETITION. I NEEDED AMSTRAM'S LETTER TO GET THE RIGHT ADDRESS.

YOU'RE RIGHT. I'M SORRY I OVERREACTED...

PHILATELLO, WE'RE NOT HERE TO BLAME ANYONE... JUST TELL US WHAT YOU KNOW!

AROBASE HAS A UNIQUE GIFT FOR COMMUNICATING WITH EVERYONE AROUND HIM. THAT'S WHY HE HAD SUCH A CLOSE RELATIONSHIP WITH HIS CARAPODE... BUT IT'S ALSO A HUGE DRAWBACK IN OUR LINE OF WORK!

A SHORT TIME BEFORE HE DISAPPEARED, I HAD AN ARGUMENT WITH AROBASE.

AROBASE LOVED TO SPEND TIME EXCHANGING NEWS WITH THE PEOPLE IN THE CITIES WE VISIT, EVEN THOUGH THAT'S WHAT LETTERS ARE FOR!

HOW'S YOUR BROTHER, MARYSE? IS HE STILL WRITING THOSE WONDERFUL POEMS?

OH, YOU REMEMBER HIM? HOW DO YOU REMEMBER EVERYONE YOU DELIVER MAIL TO?

THAT'S ENOUGH, AROBASE!

WE'RE ALREADY RUNNING LATE! OUR JOB IS NOT TO MAKE FRIENDS WITH PEOPLE BUT TO DELIVER THEIR MAIL. YOU'RE ENDANGERING THE WHOLE CARAPOST WITH YOUR DELAYS!

OUR MISSION IS TO CREATE A SOCIAL NETWORK AMONG ALL THE PEOPLE WHO LIVE ON THIS PLANET. I THOUGHT YOU UNDERSTOOD THAT AS MUCH AS I DO.

I DIDN'T THINK THAT HE'D HOLD A GRUDGE AGAINST ME. I UNDERSTAND HIS POINT OF VIEW, BUT I WAS ONLY DOING MY JOB...

YOUR ARGUMENT WASN'T THE ONLY REASON HE LEFT. THE SNAKE TOOK ADVANTAGE OF THE SITUATION FOR HIS OWN EVIL PURPOSES. WE'RE LEAVING FOR QWERTUS RIGHT AWAY TO BRING AROBASE BACK.

BUT YOU SEE, THEIR LOVE WAS TOO STRONG, AND DESPITE THE HATRED AND CONFLICT BETWEEN THEIR FAMILIES, THEY DECIDED TO RUN AWAY TOGETHER THAT VERY NIGHT.
ABOVE THE SLEEPING CITY HUNG A BEAUTIFUL FULL MOON...

TAKING ADVANTAGE OF THE BRIGHT MOONLIGHT, THEY JUMPED FROM THE CLIFF ONTO THE BACK OF A WILD CARAPODE WHO WAS PASSING BELOW THEM. FROM THEN ON, THEY MADE THEIR HOME ON THIS ANIMAL. AND SOME MONTHS LATER...

THEIR LOVE WAS SEALED BY THE ARRIVAL OF A LITTLE SON. AND SO ALL THREE OF THEM LIVED HAPPILY EVER AFTER, FAR FROM THE TUMULT OF AZERTUS...

WONDERFUL! I'M SO HAPPY I CAME!
YES! I'M GLAD AROBASE ISN'T IN THE JOKE COMPETITION-- THAT WOULD BE A CARA-STROPHE FOR ME!
WE DIDN'T MAKE THIS LONG TRIP TO QWERTUS JUST TO ADMIRE HIS TALENTS, DID WE?

LET'S HAVE A BIG ROUND OF APPLAUSE FOR OUR STORYTELLER-- AROBASE!
YOU'RE RIGHT, FOX, BUT LET HIM HAVE HIS MOMENT IN THE SPOTLIGHT.

AROBASE? DO YOU HAVE A FEW MOMENTS TO SPEAK WITH US?

I'M THE LITTLE PRINCE, AND THESE ARE MY FRIENDS, FOX AND AMSTRAM. WE'VE COME TO--
WE'VE COME FROM PHILATELLO! EVER SINCE YOU ABANDONED YOUR POST, HE AND THE OTHERS HAVE BEEN STUCK IN THE DESERT!

OF COURSE! I ALWAYS ENJOY LISTENING TO PEOPLE!

AMSTRAM! AROBASE IS UNDER THE SNAKE'S INFLUENCE!

IT MAKES NO DIFFERENCE, LITTLE PRINCE. AMSTRAM IS RIGHT. I WAS JUST BEING SELFISH WHEN I LEFT ALL MY FRIENDS IN THE DESERT...

WHY DID YOU DECIDE TO LEAVE?
IF YOU SAW MY SHADOW-PUPPET PLAY, YOU ALREADY KNOW THE ANSWER...

PEOPLE WHO LIVE IN DIFFERENT CITIES HAD ONLY BEEN ABLE TO SEE ONE ANOTHER ONCE A YEAR, DURING THE GOLDEN WEEK.

EVEN WHEN THE FIVE BIG CITIES WEREN'T AT WAR, THEY NEVER REALLY COMMUNICATED WITH ONE ANOTHER. WE DIDN'T KNOW OUR NEIGHBORS, AND FEAR ALWAYS COMES FROM THE UNKNOWN. MY FATHER WORRIED THAT THIS IGNORANCE WOULD EVENTUALLY TURN INTO HATRED, AND EVIL WOULD FOLLOW.

TO PREVENT THIS EVIL, HE WANTED TO FORGE A BOND AMONG THE CITIES. MY FATHER AND MOTHER, WHO WERE FROM DIFFERENT CITIES, DECIDED TO FORM A UNION THAT WOULD LEAD PEOPLE TO REALIZE THAT ESTABLISHING FRIENDSHIPS WITH PEOPLE FROM OTHER CITIES WAS THE KEY TO OUR FUTURE HAPPINESS...

AT THE END OF ONE GOLDEN WEEK, MY PARENTS DARED THE IMPOSSIBLE BY JUMPING ONTO THE BACK OF A WILD CARAPODE.

THE CARAPODE WAS DEEPLY MOVED BY THEIR BRAVE DEED AND BROUGHT THEM TO A SAFE PLACE.

AND SO I WAS BORN AMONG THE WILD CARAPODES. AS I GREW UP WITH THEM, I GOT TO KNOW AND UNDERSTAND THEM. MY PARENTS DECIDED TO ESTABLISH THE CARAPOST, AND IT'S PERFECTLY NATURAL FOR ME TO FOLLOW IN THEIR FOOTSTEPS.

BUT THROUGH THE YEARS, THE CARAPOST BEGAN TO CHANGE. NOWADAYS, THE ONLY THING THAT COUNTS IS DELIVERING THE MAIL ON TIME. WHAT'S IN THE LETTERS AND THE STORIES THEY TELL DON'T SEEM TO MATTER.

LITTLE BY LITTLE, I FELT THAT I WAS BETRAYING WHAT MY PARENTS SET OUT TO DO. THE CARAPOST HAD BECOME TOO EFFICIENT AND IMPERSONAL. PEOPLE STOPPED WRITING LONG, THOUGHTFUL LETTERS. AS I JOURNEYED FROM CITY TO CITY, I TRIED TO HELP PEOPLE FEEL CONNECTED TO ONE ANOTHER...

I WAS NAIVE. ALL I MANAGED TO DO WAS SLOW DOWN THE DELIVERY OF MAIL. PHILATELLO WAS RIGHT TO POINT OUT THAT I WAS ENDANGERING THE WHOLE FABRIC OF OUR SOCIETY. I FACED AN IMPOSSIBLE DILEMMA.

THAT'S WHEN THE SNAKE APPEARED. HE TRIED TO CONVINCE ME THAT ABANDONING THE CARAPOST WAS THE RIGHT THING TO DO AND WOULD MAKE ME HAPPY.

I BELIEVED THE SNAKE. I CONVINCED MYSELF THAT IT WOULD BE MORE USEFUL TO SPREAD MY PARENTS' MESSAGE ACROSS THE WORLD BY TELLING THEIR STORY...

...EVEN AT THE PRICE OF STOPPING THE MAIL. I MADE MY CHOICE AND I DON'T REGRET IT. BUT I MISS MY CARAPODE SO MUCH.

FOR ONCE, I HAVE TO ADMIT THAT THE SNAKE'S ARGUMENTS MAKE A LITTLE BIT OF SENSE. IT'S IMPORTANT TO FOLLOW YOUR DREAMS...

BUT IF THE CARAPOST DOESN'T START UP AGAIN, THIS PLANET'S IN TROUBLE. HAVING GOOD INTENTIONS ISN'T ENOUGH--
BEING A GROWN-UP MEANS FULFILLING YOUR RESPONSIBILITIES. SOMETIMES WE HAVE TO DO THINGS WE DON'T WANT TO DO. AROBASE SHOULD DO WHAT'S BEST FOR EVERYBODY ELSE EVEN IF IT MAKES HIM UNHAPPY.

FOX...

I JUST WANT TO BE AN ARTIST AND USE MY TALENTS TO THE BEST OF MY ABILITY. BUT THE CARAPOST MAKES THAT IMPOSSIBLE!

AROBASE, THERE ARE MANY PEOPLE WHO LIVE THROUGH THEIR LETTERS AND USE THEM TO EXPLAIN HOW THEY FEEL. MY SON IS WAITING FOR MAIL FROM HIS SWEETHEART. HE AND A LOT OF OTHER PEOPLE LIKE HIM ARE COUNTING ON YOU!

WHAT? NO PUNS?

YOU'RE RIGHT. I'VE MADE A MISTAKE. I'LL COME WITH YOU. JUST GIVE ME TIME TO LET THE CIRCUS KNOW.

ARCHIBALD, MY OLD FRIEND, I THINK OUR NEW STORYTELLER IS BRINGING OUR CIRCUS BACK TO ITS FORMER GLORY!

ZIG, MAY I SPEAK WITH YOU?
OF COURSE, AROBASE. I ALWAYS HAVE TIME FOR OUR NEW STAR!

I'VE BEEN HAPPIER HERE THAN I CAN EVER SAY. YOU'VE BEEN SO KIND TO ME. BUT I'M AFRAID THAT I HAVE TO GO BACK TO WORKING FOR THE CARAPOST. I'M SO SORRY.

BUT...BUT WHY? IF YOU'RE SO HAPPY HERE, WHY GO BACK TO BEING SO MISERABLE?

I'VE REALIZED I ALREADY WAS HAPPY, ZIG. SOMETIMES YOU DON'T SEE THE VALUE OF SOMETHING UNTIL YOU GIVE IT UP. I MISS MY CARAPODE, I MISS THE PEOPLE OF THE CITIES, AND MOST OF ALL, I UNDERSTAND NOW JUST HOW USEFUL I CAN BE TO THEM.

THANKS FOR EVERYTHING. I HOPE I'LL BE ABLE TO SEE YOU WHEN THE CARAPOST VISITS QWERTUS AGAIN...
I UNDERSTAND... I CAN'T KEEP YOU HERE AGAINST YOUR WILL. TAKE CARE OF YOURSELF.

HSSS... YOU'RE NOT JUST GOING TO LET HIM LEAVE, ARE YOU? HSSS...ESPECIALLY WHEN YOUR CIRCUS IS STARTING TO REGAIN ITS LOST GLORY? HSSS...
WHO... WHO ARE YOU?

IT DOESN'T MATTER... HSSS...I ONLY WANT TO HELP YOU SSSUCCEED...

I CAN'T FORCE AROBASE TO STAY.

HSSS...THINK ABOUT IT. HIS NEW FRIENDS ARE A BAD INFLUENCE ON HIM. YOU CAN FREE YOUR FRIEND FROM A MISERABLE JOB AND MAKE YOURSELF RICH AT THE SAME TIME!

HSSS...YOU COULD SSSIMPLY SSSCARE HIS NEW FRIENDS INTO LEAVING AROBASE ALONE.

YES...YOU ARE ABSOLUTELY RIGHT. THANK YOU FOR YOUR ADVICE.

ARCHIBALD! CHASE THE STRANGERS AWAY SO THEY'LL STOP BOTHERING YOUR FRIEND AROBASE!

GRRRROWL...

GRRROWR?
ARCHIBALD MAY NOT BE FIERCE ENOUGH...HE'S MUCH BETTER AT DOING TRICKS!

HSSS... I HAVE JUST WHAT HE NEEDS... HSSS...

GRRRRROWWRR?

WHAT HAVE YOU DONE TO ARCHIBALD?
I DID WHAT HAD TO BE DONE. HSSS...

WHAT KIND OF ANIMAL WOULD YOU LIKE TO RIDE BACK TO THE CARAPOST?
I VOTE FOR A CARA-BOU!
GRAOOAAARRR!

WHAT'S THAT?

GRRAAAORGGH!
THE GLOOMIES!

STAND BACK!

ARCHIBALD IS INSIDE THE MONSTER! TRY NOT TO HURT HIM!

I'LL DEAL WITH HIM!

ALL RIGHT...
YOU GET INSIDE! I'LL DRAW HIS ATTENTION!

WHAT'S HE DOING? WHY DOESN'T HE DEFEND HIMSELF?
HE'D RATHER SACRIFICE HIMSELF THAN HURT ARCHIBALD!

NOOOOO!

GRRRRR! I'LL MAKE YOU PAY FOR WHAT YOU'VE DONE.

STOP! YOU HAVE NO CHANCE AGAINST IT...

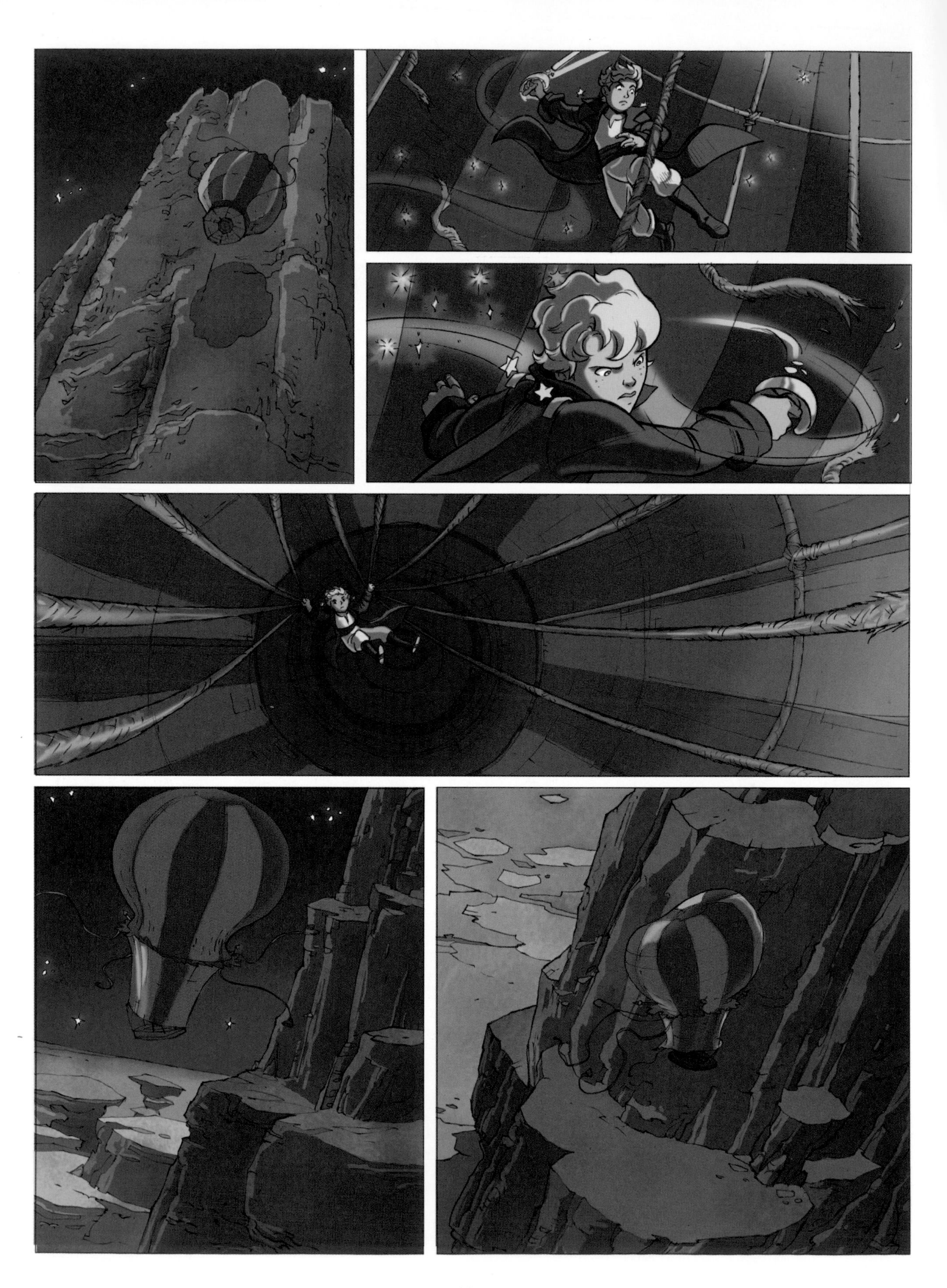

ARE YOU ALL RIGHT, FOX?
YES... BUT I REALLY NEED TO LEARN CARA-TE!

WE'RE DOOMED...

QUICK, JUMP!

I THOUGHT I'D NEVER SEE YOU AGAIN!
WELL, YOU KEEP TELLING ME TO IMPROVE MY SENSE OF HUMOR!

WHAT HAVE I DONE? WHAT WILL BECOME OF ARCHIBALD?
DON'T WORRY, ZIG. WE'LL FIND THE CARAPOST AND FIX EVERYTHING!

A TORNADO! WE'RE TOO LATE.
I'M GOING TO TRY TO LAND ON THE CARAPOST. WE'VE GOT TO MAKE THE CARAPODE MOVE BEFORE THE TORNADO ARRIVES!
NOW!

OH NO, THE LETTERS!

GRAB THEM BEFORE WE LOSE THEM ALL!

WE MADE IT...
...AND WE BROUGHT AROBASE BACK WITH US.

BUT WE'VE FAILED IN OUR DUTY. WE'LL NEVER RETRIEVE ALL THE LETTERS!
DON'T GIVE UP HOPE! AROBASE CAN MOVE US TO SAFETY. WE HAVE TO BELIEVE IN HIM!

AROBASE, GET YOUR CARAPODE MOVING. WE HAVE TO ESCAPE THE TORNADO. THE REST OF YOU, GRAB AS MANY LETTERS AS YOU CAN!
MY INVITATION MIGHT BE LOST?
CATCH WHAT YOU CAN!

OOOOF...MY INVITATION!

I NEVER SHOULD HAVE LEFT YOU, MY FRIEND. BUT IT'S TIME FOR US TO GO...TOGETHER!

IT'S THE CARAPOST! THEY'RE BACK!

I HATE TO THINK HOW DISAPPOINTED THEY'LL BE WHEN WE TELL THEM WE HAVE NO LETTERS FOR THEM.

HURRAH! HURRAH!

I JUST CAN'T BRING MYSELF TO TELL THEM...
I HAVE AN IDEA...

MY FELLOW KESKIS, THE TECHNICAL DIFFICULTIES THAT DELAYED THE CARAPOST HAVE BEEN CORRECTED...

SADLY, WE WERE OVERTAKEN BY A STORM IN THE DESERT, AND ALL THE LETTERS WERE LOST...

SO...WE'VE WAITED ALL THIS TIME FOR NOTHING? WE'LL NEVER FIND OUT HOW OUR FRIENDS ARE DOING?

WE MAY NOT HAVE ANY LETTERS, BUT AROBASE HAS A MARVELOUS TALENT FOR LISTENING TO OTHERS AND REMEMBERING WHAT THEY SAY. LET HIM GIVE YOU THE NEWS!

DO YOU... THINK I CAN?
OF COURSE! IT'S WHAT YOU DO BEST, AROBASE. TELL THEM ABOUT THEIR LOVED ONES!

WELL, AMBROSIA, WHEN YOUR SON CAME TO DROP OFF HIS MAIL, HE WAS WEARING A MAGNIFICENT PURPLE OUTFIT, EMBROIDERED WITH A GOLDEN SUN...
SO...THAT MEANS MY SON PASSED HIS TEST! YOU HEAR? HE PASSED HIS TEST!

WHAT ABOUT MY FATHER? HAVE YOU HEARD FROM HIM? HE'S BEEN BEDRIDDEN FOR MONTHS!
HE BROUGHT HIS MAIL TO ME, STUCK ONTO HIS CANE...HE LIMPS, BUT HE CAN GET AROUND!

HAVE YOU SEEN MY AUNT? HOW'S MY SON-IN-LAW? DO YOU KNOW IF MY DAUGHTER HAD HER BABY?
THANKS, AMSTRAM. I KNOW YOU DID WHAT YOU COULD TO BRING BACK THE CARAPOST. WE MAY NOT HAVE LETTERS, BUT AT LEAST WE HAVE HOPE.

PAPA...?
WELL, GRAMM, I THINK YOU'RE WAITING FOR NEWS FROM SOMEONE, AREN'T YOU?

WE MISSED YOU AT THE PARTY IN HONOR OF THE CARAPOST.

FORGIVE ME... MY THOUGHTS ARE ELSEWHERE...

YOU'RE THINKING ABOUT ARCHIBALD AND THE CIRCUS PERFORMERS BACK IN QWERTUS, AREN'T YOU?
I'M SORRY... I KNOW I BELONG WITH THE CARAPOST, BUT I'LL MISS THE CIRCUS SO MUCH!

I THINK WE'VE COME UP WITH A SOLUTION...
WHAT IF ZIG STARTS A TRAVELING CIRCUS THAT ACCOMPANIES THE CARAPOST? WE COULD CALL IT THE CARA-VAN-- LETTERS, STORIES, AND A CIRCUS ALL IN ONE!

BRILLIANT!

WELL, IT'S ABOUT TIME FOR US TO LEAVE, DON'T YOU THINK?

I HOPE WE CAN LOOK IN ON THEM FROM TIME TO TIME.
WE CAN USE YOUR CAR-EIDOSCOPE!

THE END

The Little Prince

AS IMAGINED BY

JACQUES LAMONTAGNE

LOOKS LIKE A PRETTY NICE PLANET.
IT REMINDS ME OF EARTH BUT MUCH SMALLER.

LOOK OVER THERE.

HELLO! WHAT ARE YOU DOING?
?

QUIET! CAN'T YOU SEE I'M BUSY!
BUSY DOING WHAT?

ISN'T IT OBVIOUS? I'M CREATING A MACHINE TO CONTROL THE SEASONS.
WHY WOULD YOU WANT TO CONTROL THE SEASONS?

WELL, IT JUST SO HAPPENS THAT I'M A GREAT SPORTSMAN.
WHAT EFFECT WOULD YOUR MACHINE HAVE ON SPORTS?
YOU COULD HAVE FOOLED ME.

I LOVE TO PLAY GOLF IN THE SUMMER, SKI IN THE WINTER, HUNT IN THE AUTUMN.
gulp
AND IN THE SPRING, I LOVE TO MATCH WITS WITH TROUT.
SO?

SO??!!
I HATE HOW NATURE DICTATES THE SEQUENCE OF THE SEASONS! I WANT TO DO WHATEVER I WANT, WHENEVER I WANT TO! THAT'S THE REASON FOR THE MACHINE!

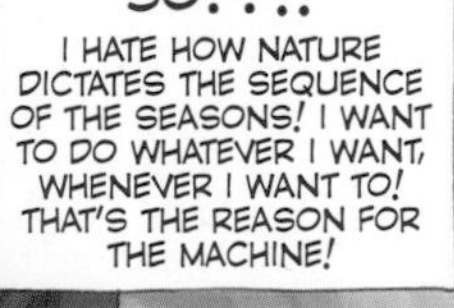
HAVE YOU BEEN WORKING ON IT FOR A LONG TIME?

AS OF TOMORROW, I WILL HAVE WORKED ON MY MACHINE, DAY AND NIGHT, FOR EXACTLY 22 YEARS.

WHAT ABOUT GOLF? AND FISHING?
ONCE I'VE FINISHED MY MACHINE, I CAN DEVOTE MYSELF TO THEM COMPLETELY.
WHEN WILL THAT BE?
I HOPE TO BE FINISHED IN 8 TO 10 YEARS.
THERE'S A FLAW IN HIS LOGIC SOMEWHERE.

MAYBE I CAN HELP. I'M AN EXPERT ON SEASON-CONTROLLING MACHINES.
WHAT? YOU NEVER TOLD ME THAT!

REALLY?!!!
OF COURSE. MOVE OVER.

HAVE YOU FOUND THE FAULT?
TOC TOC
BANG

GOT IT! YOU'LL BE DONE IN NO TIME. ALL YOU NEED ARE A FEW ADJUSTMENTS.

FROM NOW ON, YOUR MACHINE WILL DECIDE EVERYTHING. NATURE WILL HAVE NO MORE CONTROL OVER THE SEASONS.

SUMMER
AUTUMN
WINTER
SPRING
I'VE SET IT FOR "SUMMER." IN THREE MONTHS, IT WILL AUTOMATICALLY SWITCH TO "AUTUMN MODE." THEN, THREE MONTHS LATER, TO "WINTER" AND, FINALLY, TO "SPRING."

YOU ARE NOW THE GRAND MASTER OF THE SEASONS, AND HENCEFORTH, YOU CAN PLAY YOUR SPORTS ACCORDING TO THE CYCLE CREATED BY YOUR INVENTION.
BUT NOTHING'S CHANGED!
SHHH.

I'M A GENIUS!! THANKS TO MY MACHINE, I NOW HAVE TOTAL CONTROL OVER MY SPORTS SCHEDULE!! THANK YOU, YOUNG SIR! BY THE WAY, WHAT IS YOUR NAME?
I'M THE LITTLE PRINCE. AND YOU?

MY NAME IS VIVALDI. GOOD-BYE, LITTLE PRINCE!
FORE!
ADULTS ARE VERY STRANGE, FOX. WHEN THEY TRY TO CONTROL EVERYTHING, THEY LOSE TRACK OF WHAT'S IMPORTANT AND LET LIFE JUST SLIP THROUGH THEIR FINGERS.
POC
LAMONTAGNE

Antoine de Saint-Exupéry

Aviator • Author • Adventurer • Hero

Antoine de Saint-Exupéry, author of the novel *The Little Prince* on which these new adventures are based, was born on June 29, 1900, in Lyon, France. He was the third of five children: Marie-Madeleine, Simone, Antoine, François, and Gabrielle. It was when he was twelve years old, during his summer break from boarding school, that airplanes and flying first made a huge impression on him.

In 1920, he was accepted into the École des Beaux-Arts in Paris to study architecture, but the next year he joined the Second Aviation Regiment of the armed forces and received his pilot's license. In 1922, he had his first plane crash and suffered a head fracture. He had to leave the armed forces and work at different jobs on the ground to earn a living.

By May of 1926, Saint-Exupéry was able to fly again. He delivered airmail, which was a new and sometimes dangerous profession, on routes from France to Senegal and all the way to South America. That was where, in 1931, he met and married Consuelo Suncin.

From 1933 to 1938, Saint-Exupéry was very busy. He traveled to North Africa and Indochina and attempted to break the flight speed record from Paris to Saigon, Vietnam—during which his plane crashed again. It went down in the middle of the Sahara Desert. After his recovery, his life became even busier. He wrote newspaper reports in Spain on the Spanish Civil War, scouted airplane routes between Casablanca and Timbuktu, wrote a screenplay, registered several patents, and traveled to the United States. In 1939, with the start of World War II, he returned to France and talked his way into a job as a high-risk reconnaissance pilot for the French Air Force. But this only lasted until France reached an armistice agreement with Germany.

In December 1940, Saint-Exupéry returned to visit friends in New York, where he finally began work on *The Little Prince.* The story is narrated by a pilot who has crashed his plane into the Sahara Desert. He meets a little prince visiting from a faraway asteroid. Along the way, the prince also meets Fox and Snake. By late 1942, after spending the spring and summer writing and illustrating, Saint-Exupéry had completed his novel, and in April 1943 it was published in his native language of French *(Le Petit Prince)* and in English.

Saint-Exupéry was eager to return to the war. He decided to join the Free French Forces in Algeria, who were continuing the fight against the Axis powers. Because of his age, at first he had a hard time convincing them to let him fly. He was authorized to fly five dangerous missions. In fact, he flew eight. On July 31, 1944, Saint-Exupéry went on a scouting flight to prepare for military landings in the south of France. His plane disappeared over the water, and he was never seen again.

Over the decades since *The Little Prince* was published, it has gone on to become one of the best-selling novels of all time. In 2003, a small moon in our solar system's asteroid belt was named Petit-Prince in honor of the masterpiece Saint-Exupéry created.

planet, the Snake sends bad thoughts into the minds of its inhabitants, making them sad and grim, draining the life out of their planet. The Little Prince must leave his beautiful Rose behind and must use his vision and courage to defeat the Snake, bringing along his friend Fox to save planets in danger across the universe.

About the Adapters

After several years in video games and Japanese animation, adapter Guillaume Dorison became literary editor for the publisher Les Humanoïdes Associés in 2006, where he launched the Shogun Collection dedicated to original manga. In June 2010, he founded Élyum Studio with Didier Poli, Jean-Baptiste Hostache, and Xavier Dorison to provide services for the creation of graphic novels. In addition to his position as director of writing for Élyum Studio, he has more than two dozen comics and manga to his credit under the pseudonym IZU, has written several titles in the Explora series on world explorers for French publisher Glénat, and won the 2010 Animeland Prize for best French manga.

Didier Poli, artistic director for the new graphic novel adaptations based on *The Little Prince*, was born in Lyon in 1971. After graduate studies in applied arts, he worked for various animation studios including Disney. He was working as artistic director for the video game company Kalisto Entertainment when he met Manuel Bichebois in 2001 and began drawing Bichebois's graphic novel series L'Enfant de l'orage. At the 2004 Nîmes Festival, Didier Poli received the Bronze Boar prize for young talent. He continues, along with his work on graphic novels, to work regularly in cartoons and video games as a designer and storyboard artist.

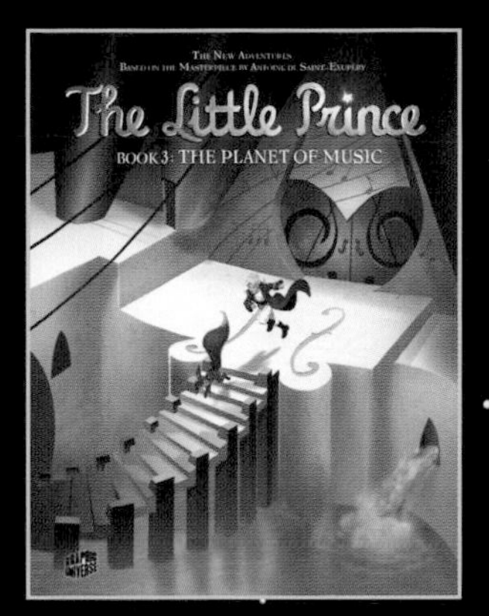

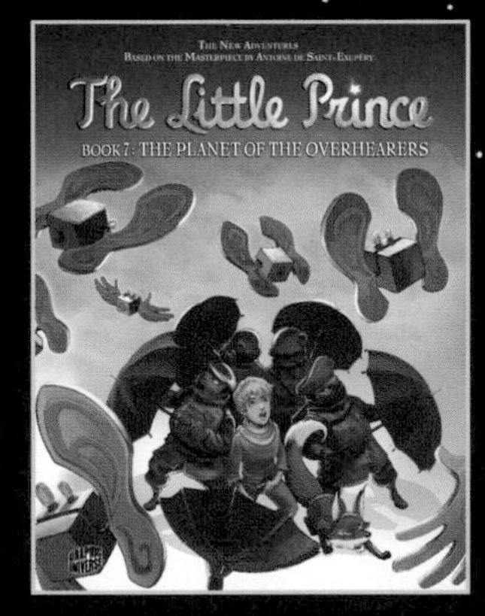

Book 1: The Planet of Wind

Book 2: The Planet of the Firebird

Book 3: The Planet of Music

Book 4: The Planet of Jade

Book 5: The Star Snatcher's Planet

Book 6: The Planet of the Night Globes

Book 7: The Planet of the Overhearers

Book 8: The Planet of the Tortoise Driver